Grandma's Secret

For Ian

PB

In memory of my mother
Alice Kovalski

MK

Kids Can Press Ltd. gratefully acknowledges the assistance of
the Canada Council and the Ontario Arts Council in the
production of this book.

Canadian Cataloguing in Publication Data

Bourgeois, Paulette
    Grandma's secret

ISBN 0-921103-57-3 (bound) ISBN 1-55074-034-2 (pbk)

I. Kovalski, Maryann. II. Title.
PS8553.087G73 1989   jC813'.54   C89-093403-7
PZ7.B67Gr 1989

Kids Can Press Ltd.,
585½ Bloor Street West,
Toronto, Ontario, Canada, M6G 1K5.

Book design by Michael Solomon
Printed and bound in Hong Kong by Everbest Co., Ltd.

PA 90 8 7 6 5 4 3 2 1

Grandma's Secret

WRITTEN BY Paulette Bourgeois
ILLUSTRATED BY Maryann Kovalski

Kids Can Press Ltd.
Toronto

My grandma lived in a pink and white house with a porch
and a picket fence. It was on the worst street in town. At
night we'd sit and watch the goings-on at the rooming house

across the street. Grandma would cross herself and mutter: "Tch, tch, tch." But every night she'd be back on the porch, rocking and watching.

Grandma didn't have any teeth. Well, that's not exactly true. She had false teeth, but she kept them in a cup full of water on a table by her bed.

She tried wearing them once. "Feels like I got me a mouth full of piano keys," she said. And she never put them in again.

Grandma didn't cook. "No need for cooking when you're an old lady with no teeth," she'd say. For breakfast my grandma had tea with sugar and milk and I had milk with tea and sugar. We ate Jell-O and thick slabs of bologna and chocolate-covered marshmallow cookies that were stored in the oven. "No need for an oven when you're an old lady with no teeth," Grandma would say. I loved being at my grandma's house. Except I worried about the bear.

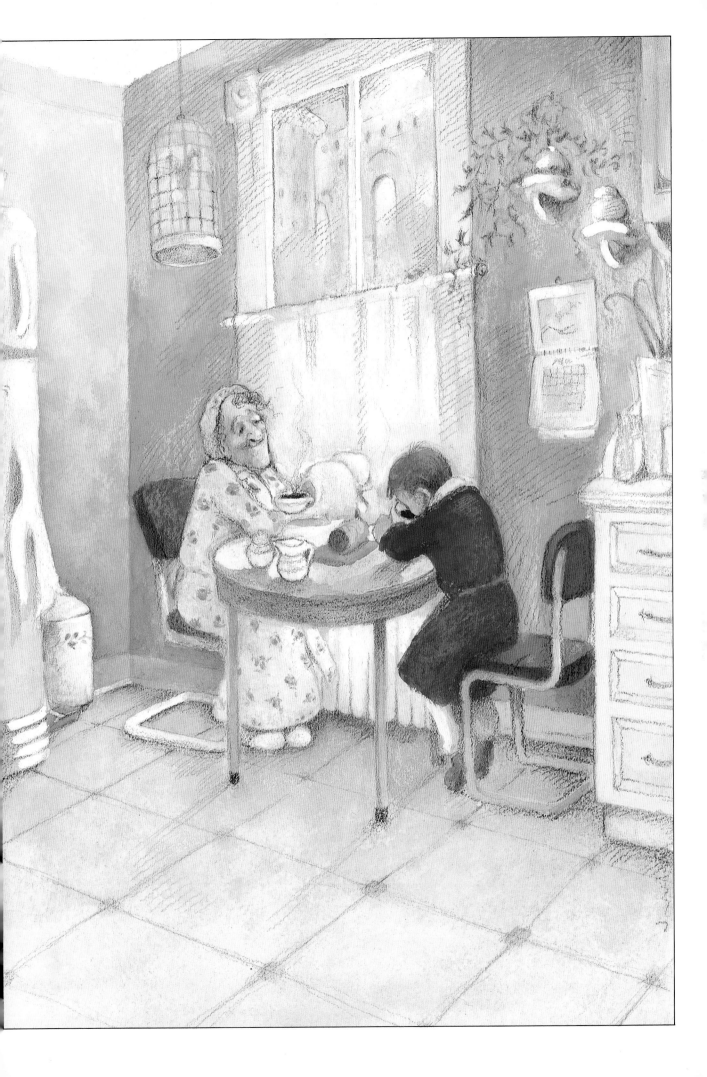

Every morning at breakfast Grandma pointed to a small door leading to the basement.

"Wouldn't open that if I were you."

"Why?"

"'Cause there's a bear down there," she'd say.

"You're making that up. There's no bear down there."

And every morning my grandma would stare straight at me, cup her hand to her ear and say: "Listen."

Sometimes I'd hear rustling like something was moving around. If I listened very carefully I'd swear I could hear something like a low growl made at the back of a throat. But I'd tell my grandma: "I don't hear anything."

"Still," she'd say, "wouldn't go down there if I were you."

And for a long time I didn't.

Our days were busy. Grandma liked the trains and so did I. She'd put on a black tam and shoes, black-velvet, high-heeled shoes with holes where her big toes peeked out. She'd wear her favourite dress, the one with the big pink flowers and buttons shaped like roses. We'd walk to the end of the street and stand under the trestle waiting for the scream of the wheels and the shudder of the bridge. When we could hear the rumble of the train, Grandma would grab my hand. If there were people around I'd jerk it back, embarrassed. "Grandma, I'm too big for holding hands," I'd hiss. But if there wasn't anybody else under the bridge, I liked the feel of her hand in mine.

When I went to school Grandma dusted. She dusted the china dogs that guarded every door and the pictures of Our Lady on all the walls. She dusted the cupboard and every piece of clear-blue china inside. We never ate off that china.

"No sense setting a fancy table when you're an old lady with no teeth," she'd say.

And at night we'd rock on the porch watching the goings-on across the street. I rocked as long as Grandma let me; I hated going to bed because of that darn bear in the basement. I'd lie in the great soft sag in my bed listening to his breath. Lift and fall, lift and fall.

HHHuuuuuuuuuuuMMMMmmmmmmmmm,
HHHHHHHuuuuuuuuuuuMMMMMMMMmmmmmmmm.

I'd hear him padding around and around and around. I'd wonder if he was chained and decided he was. I mean if he wasn't, he'd come upstairs, wouldn't he? I'd wonder who fed him — Grandma never went down those stairs. I spent my nights under the flickering sign that said "Hotel Alexandra," wondering and listening. Until one night when I couldn't wonder or listen anymore.

   I crept past my grandma's bedroom and peeked in to make
sure she was asleep. She looked so small in the folds of her
comforter. And her hair was crimped tightly around pieces of
tissue and pins.

I stayed a long time. I think I wanted her to wake up and
say, "Wouldn't go down there if I were you."
But she didn't, so I kept walking. Past the china guard
dogs, past the pink china cupboard into the kitchen.

The door to the basement wasn't even locked. I groped for the switch and flicked it. The bulb hanging from a socket at the bottom of the stairs didn't cast much light, but the Hotel Alexandra sign flickered through the basement windows, too.

I listened from the top of the steps but all I heard was the thumping in my chest. The steps had rotted from the dampness in the air and one good shove could have toppled the railing. The stairs were so steep I had to lean forward and peer over my toes just to see the next step.

Then I saw him. Geez, he was huge. His jaws were open and he was standing on two hind legs ready to attack. But he wasn't moving. He wasn't even stuffed. The bear in the basement was cardboard.

I sat down on the last of those steep rotted steps. It was better not knowing, not knowing for sure, about the bear in the basement. My grandma was right, I shouldn't have come down.

I suppose if I were an old lady with no teeth I'd try to scare the daylights out of a kid like me, too. I mean those steps were really bad. You could kill yourself going down those steps.

The hotel sign was still flickering when I climbed
carefully up the stairs. I closed the door to the basement all

the way. This time I was really quiet walking past my
grandma's door.

At breakfast the next morning my grandma had tea with sugar and milk and I had milk with tea and sugar. And then she pointed to the basement door and said:

"Wouldn't open that if I were you."

"Why?" I asked.

"'Cause there's a bear down there."

"You're making that up," I said.

And just like always my grandma said, "Listen." And I did, but all I heard was a little rumbling in the furnace and a little rustling of the wind.

"I don't hear anything," I said.

"Still," said Grandma, "wouldn't go down there if I were you."
And I didn't. That night after we'd rocked and watched
the goings-on and I went to bed, I didn't wonder if the bear
was chained. I wondered where my grandma got a
cardboard bear, anyway.